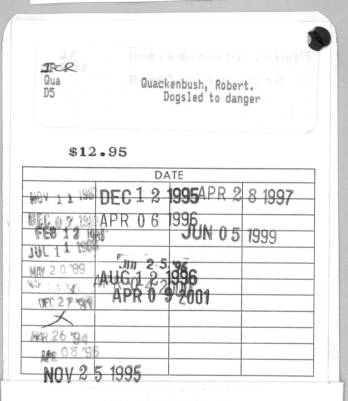

JR
Qua
D5

Quackenbush, Robert.
Dogsled to danger

$12.95

DATE		
NOV 1 1 1987	DEC 1 2 1995	APR 2 8 1997
DEC 0 2 1988	APR 0 6 1996	
FEB 1 2 1988		JUN 0 5 1999
JUL 1 1 1988		
MAY 2 0 '89	JUN 2 5 '96	
MAR 1 4 '91	AUG 1 2 1996	
DEC 2 7 '91	APR 0 9 2001	
X		
MAR 26 '94		
APR 08 '95		
NOV 2 5 1995		

Robert Quackenbush

DOGSLED TO DREAD

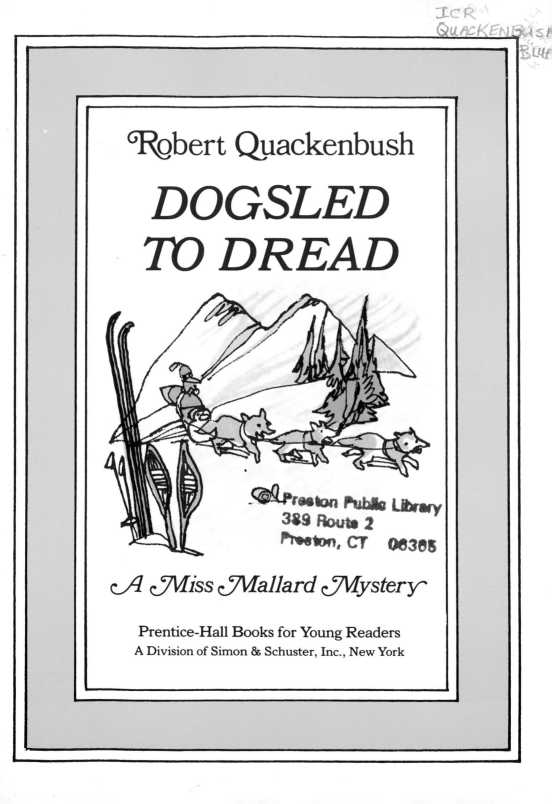

A Miss Mallard Mystery

Prentice-Hall Books for Young Readers
A Division of Simon & Schuster, Inc., New York

Published by Prentice-Hall Books for Young Readers
A Division of Simon & Schuster, Inc.
Simon & Schuster Building
Rockefeller Center
1230 Avenue of the Americas
New York, NY 10020

10   9   8   7   6   5   4   3   2   1

Prentice-Hall Books for Young Readers
is a trademark of Simon & Schuster, Inc.
Printed in Spain

Library of Congress Cataloging in Publication Data
Quackenbush, Robert M.
    Dogsled to dread.
    Summary: When Miss Mallard, the famous ducktective,
is invited to Alaska to see the start of the famous
dog sled race, her skills are challenged by the
dognapping of a prize husky.
    [1. Ducks—Fiction.   2. Alaska—Fiction.
3. Mystery and detective stories]   I. Title.
PZ7.Q16Do   1987   [Fic]   86-25394
ISBN 0-13-217225-9

For Piet and Margie

and especially for the
schoolchildren I visited
in Anchorage, Alaska

R.Q.

$\mathcal{M}$iss Mallard, the world-famous ducktective, looked up at the enormous stuffed polar bear in the lounge of the lodge where she was staying.

She shivered and said to Vera and Arnold Drake, "I can't get over the huge size of things here in Alaska. It is all so rustic and beautiful—it's like going back to the old frontier days. Thank you so much for inviting me here."

"We're so glad you could come," said Vera, who was knitting a long woolen scarf. "As the heads of the Chamber of Commerce here in Duckton, Arnold and I have been working a long time to get you here. We were grateful you could change your plans at the last minute."

"We couldn't think of a better duck to launch the dogsled races tomorrow," said Arnold. "Duckton's annual races draw a bigger crowd than the races held in Anchorage. There will be a lot of news coverage."

"How exciting!" said Miss Mallard. "I launched a ship once, but never a dogsled race."

They looked out the large picture window at the huskies and their trainers gathering outside. This was their last chance to practice for the races the following day.

"See the husky with her puppies?" Vera pointed outside. "That's Nina. She has won every race for the past three years. She is sure to win again this year. She has been friskier than ever since her puppies were born."

Miss Mallard watched the mother husky being buckled in. She was the lead dog for her sled. Her puppies were playing in the snow nearby.

Suddenly, a costumed figure on skis came tearing down the mountain. It swooped to grab a puppy and then vanished into the woods.

"Great tundra!" cried Arnold. "One of Nina's puppies has been dognapped! Quick, Vera, call Sheriff Ruddy-Duck!"

In her haste to get to a phone, Vera dropped her knitting. Miss Mallard helped her to pick it up and shove it into a bag. Then Miss Mallard grabbed her own knitting bag, where she kept her detective tools. She ran outside with Arnold.

Outside, there was confusion everywhere. Nina and the other huskies were howling and barking. Their trainers were racing around quacking and trying to calm them.

"The Totem Avenger has struck again!" cried one of the trainers.

Miss Mallard asked Arnold, "Who is the Totem Avenger?"

Arnold answered, "Months ago he sent a note to our sheriff. He said he would make everyone pay for some wrong that had been done. Ever since, he has been terrorizing our town. He wears the costume of a totem pole. One time he ruined a hockey match by sprinkling salt on the ice—the players kept tripping and falling. He has done much more—all of it bad—but this is the worst."

Just then, Sheriff Ruddy-Duck arrived in his snowmobile. News of the dognapping had spread all over town, and a crowd gathered around him. He questioned the witnesses and made out a report.

"What are you going to do about this, Sheriff?" asked Ben Scoter, Nina's trainer.

"I'll send out an all points bulletin right away on Nina's puppy," answered Sheriff Ruddy-Duck. "I will do everything I can to arrest the Totem Avenger."

With that, he put away his notebook and sped off.

After the sheriff left, Ben Scoter turned to the crowd and said, "Did you hear that? The sheriff has been talking about a speedy arrest for months. But nothing has been done to stop the Totem Avenger. I say it is time we got a new sheriff in Duckton. The one for the job is Arnold Drake. At least he and Vera brought Miss Mallard here to work on the case."

"Good idea!" said some Arnold supporters.

Miss Mallard was surprised.

"Is it true?" she asked Vera and Arnold. "Is that the real reason you invited me to Alaska?"

They both blushed and nodded their heads.

"But we still want you to start the race tomorrow," said Arnold.

"We believed you might think that our troubles in Duckton were not important enough," said Vera. "We thought if we invited you as our guest to the races, you would be more likely to come."

"Every case is important to me," said Miss Mallard.

"Then you'll help us?" said Vera and Arnold together.

"Yes," said Miss Mallard. "I'll begin my investigation at once."

"Hooray for Miss Mallard!" shouted the crowd.

Then one of Arnold's supporters said, "Let's go to the lodge and make plans for Arnold to take over as sheriff. Lead the way, Arnold!"

Vera and Arnold led the way. The crowd followed them to the lodge, chanting, "Arnold Drake for sheriff! Arnold Drake for sheriff!"

Miss Mallard stayed behind with the huskies and their trainers. Ben Scoter was at her side.

She asked Ben, "Why do you think the Totem Avenger took one of Nina's puppies?"

"For only one reason," said Ben. "You can see how upset Nina is. She will be in no shape to run in the race tomorrow unless her puppy is found. If the puppy isn't found—and I have my doubts that it will be—then the other favored team is bound to win."

"Which team is that?" asked Miss Mallard.

"George Scaup's team," said Ben.

"Are you implying that George Scaup might have had something to do with what happened here today?" Miss Mallard asked him.

"It seems pretty obvious to me," Ben replied.

George Scaup, who had been hiding behind a totem pole, ran toward them.

"I heard that, Ben!" he quacked. "I could sue you for slander, you know. I was here the whole time and you know it!"

"You could have hired someone," said Ben accusingly.

"That does it!" said George. He started to take a swing at Ben.

"GENTLEMEN!" Miss Mallard said firmly as she stood between the two. "Nina's puppy will never be found this way."

Grumbling, George went back to his huskies. Ben tried to calm poor Nina who was howling mournfully over the loss of her puppy.

Miss Mallard went to the spot where Nina's puppy had been grabbed. There were no clues. Even the Totem Avenger's ski tracks had been quickly covered by the falling snow.

But wait! One of the other puppies was tugging on something that lay half-buried in the snow. It was a woolen glove like the kind the Totem Avenger had been wearing. No doubt he had dropped it and in all the confusion no one had noticed it.

The puppy finally freed the glove. Carrying it to Miss Mallard, he laid it at her feet.

"Thank you," she said.

Miss Mallard examined the glove. It was hand-made. Maybe it came from the gift shop at the lodge, she thought. She went to investigate.

Inside the gift shop, she could hear loud talking from the lounge next door. It sounded as if Arnold would soon be the new sheriff.

Miss Mallard showed the glove to a salesperson. She asked if it had come from the shop.

"No," was the answer. "We don't carry hand-crafted items. Try Jed Merganzer's gift shop—it's called 'Welcome'—or the Portage Glacier Gift Shop. They are both within walking distance down the mountain. But you will have to wear snowshoes to get there."

"Thank you," said Miss Mallard as she left the shop.

Outside, she put on a pair of the snowshoes that were kept near the entrance of the lodge.

She braced herself against the cold wind and trudged down the mountain. At last she came to a crooked little house. The large sign over the front door said WELCOME.

"This must be Jed Merganzer's shop," said Miss Mallard.

She took off her snowshoes and walked in.

Inside, the walls of the little house were covered with scraps of paper. Old postcards, business cards, photos, and letters were pinned up all over. What a mess!, thought Miss Mallard. Then she saw someone sitting behind a counter that displayed local handicrafts.

"Are you Jed Merganzer?" asked Miss Mallard.

"Yep," said Jed. "What can I do for you?"

Miss Mallard held up the mysterious glove.

"I thought you might recognize this," she said. "Did it come from your store?"

"Never saw it before," said Jed.

Miss Mallard turned to leave.

"Pin your card on the wall," said Jed. "Everyone else does."

Miss Mallard took out a business card. "I'll pin it under this photo," she said. "I know the couple in this picture—Vera and Arnold Drake. I guess nearly everybody has been in your store."

"That's right," said Jed sourly. "But most of them don't buy anything. I wish I had a dollar for every card folks have pinned up here. I would be a rich duck."

Miss Mallard thought he sounded angry and sad. She finished pinning up her card, said goodbye, and hurriedly left.

Back in the cold, Miss Mallard put on her snowshoes and started off again.

After only a few steps, she thought she heard the faint sound of something moving. The sound came from a shed behind Jed's store.

She listened again. This time she heard a loud CRUNCH! CRUNCH! CRUNCH! She looked behind her and gasped. It was a huge moose!

"Nice moose," Miss Mallard whispered fearfully. Then she turned to run.

She clumped, clumped in her snowshoes as fast as she could. The moose was close at her heels. At last, she came to the Portage Glacier Gift Shop. She ran inside and slammed the door.

"No snowshoes inside," said the clerk in the shop.

"Sorry," said Miss Mallard. "I was being chased by a moose. I'll leave as soon as he is gone. In the meantime, do you sell this kind of glove here?"

Once more she held up the mysterious glove.

"Absolutely not!" said the clerk.

Miss Mallard looked out the window. The moose was gone.

"Then I'll be on my way," she said.

As she went out the door, she heard the clerk heave a sigh of relief.

Discouraged, Miss Mallard started back to the lodge. She stuffed the mysterious glove deep into her knitting bag. From the bottom of the bag, some strands of yarn stuck to her own mitten. She looked at them in surprise.

"I never knit," she said. "Where in the world...?"

Then she remembered. She held the yarn next to the glove she had found. They matched exactly!

Suddenly everything was clear to Miss Mallard. She ran back to the gift shop and went inside.

"This is an emergency!" she said. "I am Margery Mallard. I must use your phone!"

The clerk was thrilled to learn that the famous ducktective was in her shop. She offered to drive Miss Mallard to the lodge in a snowmobile after she telephoned.

They arrived in a whirl of snow. Miss Mallard parked her snowshoes and ran into the lounge. The last ballots were just being counted to elect Arnold the new sheriff of Duckton.

"Hold everything!" said Miss Mallard. "This election must stop. The Totem Avenger has been unmasked."

"What do you mean?" asked Vera and Arnold, puzzled.

"You will find out in just one minute," replied Miss Mallard.

All at once, a squad of snowmobiles pulled up. Out popped Sheriff Ruddy-Duck and his deputies. They had with them Jed Merganzer and Nina's puppy!

The crowd was wild with excitement and curiosity. They wanted to know what had happened.

"Without Miss Mallard," said Sheriff Ruddy-Duck, "this case might not have been solved. She called and told me where to find the puppy. And she says Jed Merganzer is the Totem Avenger. How do you know, Miss Mallard?"

"A bit of yarn did the trick," said Miss Mallard.

As soon as she said that, Vera and Arnold started to leave.

"Stop them, Sheriff," said Miss Mallard. "They are involved in this, too."

When the crowd quieted down, Miss Mallard said, "Here is the glove the Totem Avenger wore. It was knitted by Vera. I learned that when I found some strands of her yarn. Then I remembered something about a photo I had seen in Jed's store. In the photo, Jed is wearing the glove."

Miss Mallard paused for breath. She went on, "Jed took Nina's puppy and hid it in his shed. But Vera and Arnold masterminded the scheme. They hired Jed to be the Totem Avenger. They even invited me here to make themselves look innocent. They wanted Arnold to be elected sheriff, so they could take over the town. All Jed wanted was money."

"Take the crooks away, deputies," said Sheriff Ruddy-Duck.

Sheriff Ruddy-Duck and Miss Mallard returned the puppy to Nina.

It was a joyful reunion. Ben Scoter and George Scaup were there. Ben said he was sorry for thinking George had anything to do with the crime and for wanting a new sheriff. All three of them shook wings and made up. Then Nina gave Miss Mallard a big, wet, sloppy kiss.

"How can we ever thank you, Miss Mallard?" asked Sheriff Ruddy-Duck.

"Nina just did," said Miss Mallard.

10|87